I Don't Have an Uncle Phil Anymore

Published by
MAGINATION PRESS
An Educational Publishing Foundation Book
American Psychological Association
750 First Street, NE
Washington, DC 20002

For more information about our books, including a complete catalog, please write to us, call 1-800-374-2721, or visit our website at www.maginationpress.com.

Editor: Darcie Conner Johnston
Art Director: Susan K. White
The text type is Palatino
Printed by R.R. Donnelley & Sons, Willard, Ohio

Library of Congress Cataloging-in-Publication Data
Pellegrino, Marjorie White. I don't have an Uncle Phil anymore /
Marjorie White Pellegrino ; illustrated by Christine Kempf.   p.   cm.
Summary: Following the unexpected death of his uncle, a boy travels
to the funeral with his extended family and begins to think about what
the event will mean for all of them.
ISBN 1-55798-559-6 (cloth)
[1. Death-Fiction. 2. Grief-Fiction. 3. Uncles-Fiction.]
I. Kempf, Christine, ill. II. Title.
CURR PZ7.P3637Iae 1998/9   98-42828
   [Fic]-dc21   CIP
                                                                                         AC

Manufactured in the United States of America
10 9 8 7 6 5 4 3 2 1

I Don't Have an Uncle Phil Anymore

WRITTEN BY

Marjorie White Pellegrino

ILLUSTRATED BY

Christine Kempf

MAGINATION PRESS • WASHINGTON, DC

For Evan and Phil—M.W.P.

For Mom and Dad—C.K.

On the way to the birthday party, Mom says she
thinks she might paint more hearts than anything
else. She likes painting hearts best because hearts remind
her of Uncle Phil, and she's worried about him.

I help Mom when she paints faces at parties. I keep the brushes clean, and when the water gets muddy with too many colors mixed together I pour it in a sink. Then I fill the jar with fresh, clear water.

I like to keep track of how many things she paints on faces. At this party, she paints two balloons, four rainbows, three paw prints, one dragon, and eight hearts. Mom is right about the hearts.

7

When we go home, Dad is there, even though he's not supposed to be. He hugs Mom and talks to her softly, and Mom starts to cry. I'm not sure what I'm supposed to do, so I go to my room and cuddle with my bear Raisin. It feels like a long time before Dad calls for me.

We sit together on the couch. Dad pulls me up on his lap
and puts his arm around Mom. "Uncle Phil didn't get better like
we thought he would," Mom says. "Uncle Phil died today.
He had to leave to go to heaven." I'm not sure I know where
heaven is, and even though I think it's a good place my
stomach flip-flops and my throat starts to hurt. Uncle Phil won't
like being so far away from Aunt Lisa and my cousin Jenny.

Mom says we're not going to sleep at home
tonight. We're going to sleep on an airplane.
I tell Mom I can't sleep on a plane.

"I'm pretty sure that you can," Mom says.
"You don't have to go to sleep right away.
We can talk about Uncle Phil and airplanes
and anything else that you want to." Right
now all I want to do is stay in Dad's lap.

It's dark when we leave for the airport.
I sit wide awake while they tell us how to
fasten our seat belts and when they bring
us pretzels and juice.

I know I won't fall asleep.

I start to think about Uncle Phil and I wonder who he'll play with in heaven. Whenever I visited New York, he played catch with me with a sparkle blue rubber ball he let me pick out at the store— a special ball that would always be just for him and me. He and I hid it in a secret place in the back of the garage. He built block towers for me and Jenny to knock down.

He carried me out into the backyard on his shoulders. We all played tag around the dogwood trees.

Mom was right about sleeping. I do fall asleep. In my dream, Uncle Phil lifts me up onto the fire truck he rides on. He lets me step into his big black boots and put on his heavy yellow rubber coat. He puts his hard helmet on my head to protect me from a pretend fire.

14

When I wake up, the sun is shining in through the
plane windows and we aren't in Arizona anymore.
Last time when we visited New York, Grandma and
Grandpa waited for us near the gate when we got off
the plane. This time no one is standing there waving
hello. After we pick up the suitcases, a friend of
my grandma's picks us up by the street. She smiles
at me a lot when I get in the car.

"I thought people would be crying,"
I say softly to Mom as we ride over
a big gray bridge.

"People will cry," she says. "But it
won't be anything to be afraid of.
It just means they love Uncle Phil
and will miss him in their lives."

Mom was right about the crying. When we get out of the car, Grandma and Grandpa and Aunt Lisa cry and hug us for a long time. All day people come in and out of the house. Still it seems lonely without Uncle Phil. When I get ready for bed, I keep forgetting that he isn't here to say goodnight.

The next morning Mrs. Rose from across the street brings a big silver pot of chicken soup. Mr. Canelli from next door delivers bread wrapped in white paper and tied with red and white string. People I don't know bring meatballs, macaroni, ham, cakes, pies, lots of cookies, and a big yellow bowl filled with fruit. I am thinking I like everything except the bananas when Mom says it's time to get ready to go to church. We are going to church for Uncle Phil. She says it's important for us to all come together to show respect and say good-bye.

We dress up in our best clothes. In church, I get to sit way up front with my whole family. The minister says a prayer, and lots of people stand up and talk about how Uncle Phil was special to them. Mom says only Uncle Phil's body is in the big wooden box up by the altar. The most important part of him, the part that makes him smile and want to hug us, that is the part that left.

After church, Mom reminds me that I am going back to the house with her cousin Susan. "We'll be back before lunch," Mom promises. They are going to the cemetery, the place we take flowers to Great Grandpa Jack. Uncle Phil's special place will be on the same hill, between the trees and the garden.

A long line of cars with their lights on follows a shiny, black van with Uncle Phil in it. It feels like a sad parade. Susan says we can ride along for a little while.

We follow the other cars past the brick firehouse where Uncle Phil took me last time I visited. It's the firehouse in my dream on the plane.

The garage doors are rolled open. Uncle Phil's bright red engine is parked out in the driveway. Firefighters stand in a line by the street, saluting Uncle Phil's parade. One firefighter is pulling a rope that rings a bell over and over and over again. The bell sounds sad, like it wishes Uncle Phil was going to stay.

Back at the house, Susan and I help Mrs. O'Toole put lots of forks and napkins and a big pile of plates on the table. It feels funny to be here without Mom and Dad, Grandma and Grandpa, Jenny and Aunt Lisa— or Uncle Phil.

Mom was right about being back before lunch. Everyone, even the firefighters in their uniforms, comes back to eat. It's like a party, only Mom isn't painting faces and people aren't really happy. Some people laugh while they're crying.

23

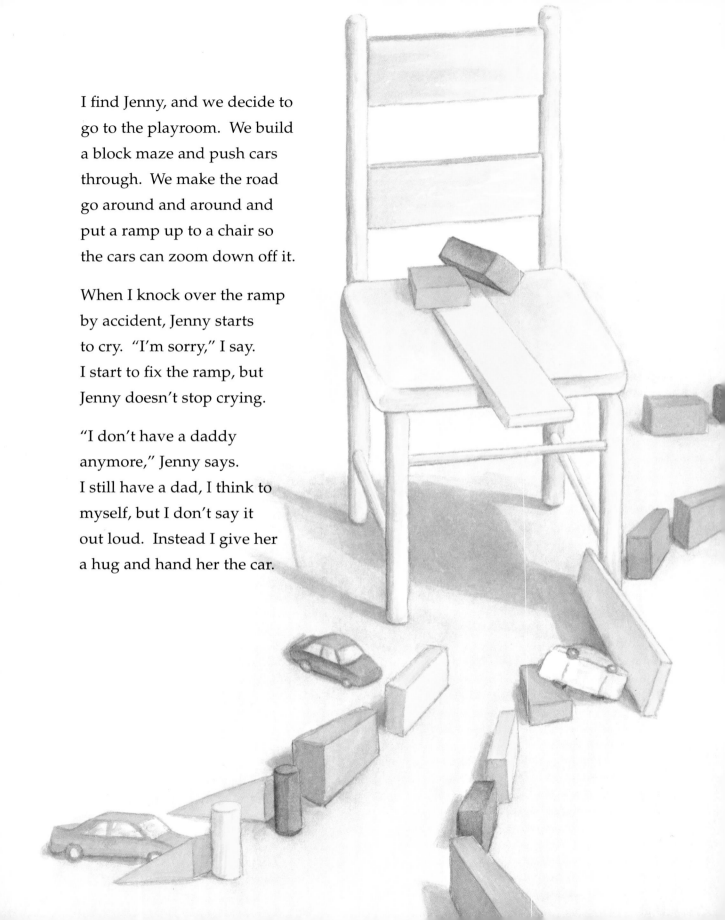

I find Jenny, and we decide to go to the playroom. We build a block maze and push cars through. We make the road go around and around and put a ramp up to a chair so the cars can zoom down off it.

When I knock over the ramp by accident, Jenny starts to cry. "I'm sorry," I say. I start to fix the ramp, but Jenny doesn't stop crying.

"I don't have a daddy anymore," Jenny says. I still have a dad, I think to myself, but I don't say it out loud. Instead I give her a hug and hand her the car.

Later, when my mom comes in to check on me, I snuggle in her arms. "I don't have an uncle anymore, huh, Mom?" I whisper, so no one else can hear. Mom whispers back that in a way I still do, only now my uncle is in heaven. I'd rather have him here to play with me.

Mom and I go outside. She pushes me on the
swings, even though I know how to pump
my legs back and forth to make the swing fly.

Mom says Uncle Phil won't get to play with
me again the way he used to. He won't be
able to lift me up onto his shoulders, or play
ball. She says he can only visit with me in my
memories and in my heart.

When Mom goes back in the house, I go into the garage. I walk to the very back behind the sled into the secret place. I take out the sparkle blue ball Uncle Phil and I hid there. I go back outside in the clear space between the dogwood trees.
I throw the ball up into the sky as high as I can.

The ball flies up into heaven.

Uncle Phil seems to catch it and throw it back down to me.

Mom wasn't quite right about Uncle Phil.